THE LITTLE RED FLOWER

For Suzie and David

By PAUL TRIPP   Illustrated by Trina Schart Hyman

THE

DOUBLEDAY & COMPANY, INC.   GARDEN CITY, NEW YORK

LITTLE RED FLOWER

Library of Congress Catalog Card Number 68-22474

Text Copyright © 1968 by Paul Tripp. Illustrations Copyright © 1968 by Trina Hyman.
All rights reserved. Printed in the United States of America. First Edition.

Nothing ever grew in the dusty coal-mining town except children.

There were no trees.

There were no flowers.

There was no grass.

Nothing ever grew in the coal-dusty town, until Mr. Green-thumb came to live there. He brought with him a little red flower in a flower pot and put it on his window sill.

The children saw it on their way home from school and stopped. They had never seen a flower before.

"What can it possibly be?" they asked each other.

"I think it's a flower," said Joseph, the doctor's son. "It looks like a picture I once saw in a book.".

The next morning, they brought their fathers and mothers
and the mayor to look at the little red thing on Mr. Greenthumb's window sill.

"We think it's a flower," said the mothers.

"It certainly *looks* like a flower," agreed the fathers.

The mayor stared at the little red flower for a very long time.

"It is a scientific fact," he said at last. "This is definitely a
flower!"

Just then the window behind the little red flower flew open and Mr. Greenthumb appeared. In one hand he held a watering can. In the other hand was a clean white cloth.

Mr. Greenthumb leaned over the little red flower and, with three whispering puffs, gently blew the dust from its red petals. Then, very carefully, he wiped the dust off each leaf with his clean white cloth.

"Did you notice that?" the people whispered to each other. "His thumb is *green!*"

The mayor nodded his head wisely.

"That explains it," he announced in a loud whisper. "They say a man with a green thumb can grow anything."

Mr. Greenthumb lifted his watering can and watered the black earth around the flower. Then he sprinkled the petals and the leaves. The little red flower sparkled in the sun.

"How wonderful!" murmured the people.

Mr. Greenthumb looked up in surprise. He had not noticed the people before.

"Please excuse us for staring," apologized the mayor, "but we've never seen a flower before."

"How very very odd!" said Mr. Greenthumb. "Would you all like to smell it?"

The people gathered around the little red flower and took a deep breath.

"Ahhhhh!" How clean and fresh it smelled.

From then on, every day seemed like a holiday to the people of the dusty town. Each morning started the same way. Mr. Greenthumb opened his window and tended to the little red flower while everyone watched.

"PFFF! PFFF! PFFF!"

WIPE! WIPE! WIPE!

SPRINKLE! SPRINKLE! SPRINKLE!

When this was done and the little red flower glistened in the sun, everybody lined up. One by one, they smelled the flower. That was the best part of all.

"Ahhhhh!"

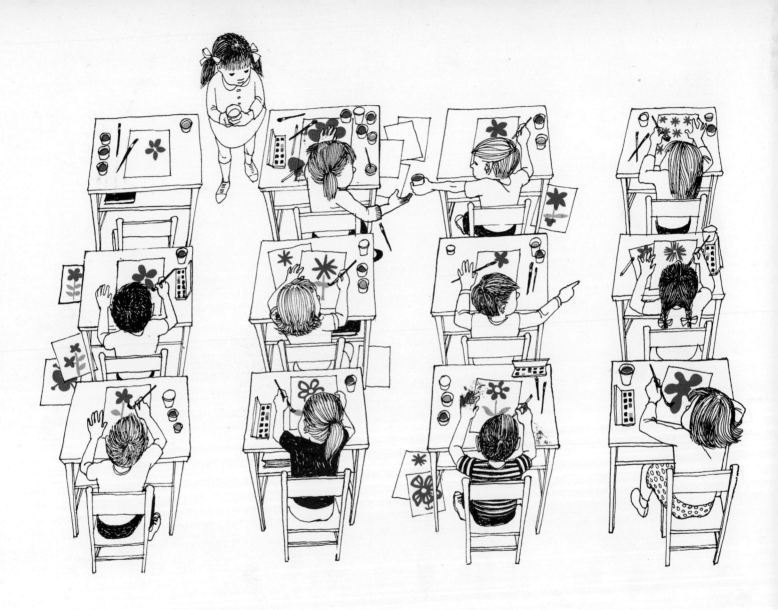

Then the children went to school and drew pictures of little red flowers.

The fathers went down into the dark mine and dug for coal. And as they swung their pickaxes, they thought about the little red flower and smiled.

The mothers went home, and while they scrubbed and cooked,
they thought of the little red flower and hummed away all day.

And each day, the mayor printed great big signs which said: THIS WAY TO OUR GARDEN. Soon every street in town had one of these signs with an arrow pointing to Mr. Greenthumb's window sill.

One morning, after everyone had smelled the flower, Mr. Greenthumb said, "I have a surprise for you. Here are some seeds for you to plant so that you can each have a little red flower of your own."

Nobody stepped forward to take the seeds he held out. Sadly, they shook their heads.

"Thank you, Mr. Greenthumb," sighed the mayor, "but planting is not for us. You are the only one who can grow a flower."

"Because you have a green thumb," added Joseph, the doctor's son.

Mr. Greenthumb stared at his green thumb and burst out laughing.

"Why bless your hearts," he chuckled, "that's not a real green thumb. When I painted my backyard fence, I stuck it into the green paint by mistake. Now the paint won't come off. This thumb has no more to do with my growing things than the fact that my name is Augustus Greenthumb. It's just a coincidence, that's all!"

But nobody believed Mr. Greenthumb. They were sure he was joking. After all, nothing had ever grown in their town before.

Only Joseph was not so sure. All day long he wondered about Mr. Greenthumb's green thumb.

Then, one hot sunny morning, Mr. Greenthumb did not appear. The families waited for his window to open. On the window sill, the little red flower waited for its morning shower. Its petals were a dusty red.

But Mr. Greenthumb did not come.

The school bell rang!

The mine whistle blew!

"Time to go!" said the mayor. And he sent everyone away.

"Don't worry," he called after them. "I'll find out what has happened to Mr. Greenthumb."

He knocked on the door. No answer!

He knocked again. The mayor shook his head, opened the door and walked into Mr. Greenthumb's house.

The forgotten little red flower stood alone in the bright sunlight.

The next moment, the door of Mr. Greenthumb's house flew open and the mayor shot out into the street, shouting, "Find the doctor! Mr. Greenthumb has a terrible fever! Where's the doctor? Find the doctor!"

There was only one doctor in the whole town. Joseph's father. He was at the school, making all the children say "AHH" when the mayor burst in.

"Come quickly, Doctor," he panted. "Mr. Greenthumb needs you."

Without another word, he grabbed the doctor's hand and ran out into the street, pulling the doctor behind him. They raced to Mr. Greenthumb's house and disappeared inside.

Meanwhile, the girls ran home to tell their mothers. And the boys ran to the mine to tell their fathers. Soon, the whole town was gathered in front of Mr. Greenthumb's house.

They waited patiently all morning. No news!

They waited nervously all afternoon. Still no news about Mr. Greenthumb.

Half the sun was down in the sky when the door finally opened and the mayor and doctor appeared, looking very tired and rumpled.

"Mr. Greenthumb is a very sick man," announced Joseph's father, "but I think I can make him better."

There was a great sigh of relief from everybody.

"But it all depends on one thing," added the doctor. "Mr. Greenthumb is very worried about his little red flower. It hasn't had any water since yesterday morning."

With a click of surprise, every head turned toward the window sill. And everybody gasped.

The little red flower wasn't red any more. Its leaves and petals were dusty gray. The earth in the pot was hard and cracked. The little flower's head drooped to one side.

The doctor peered at it through his glasses.

"*That* is a very sick flower!"

"Can't you do something for it?" asked the mayor. "After all, you are a doctor."

The doctor shook his head. "I'm a people doctor. Not a flower doctor. If you want *me* to make Mr. Greenthumb better, *you* will have to save his little flower."

He went back into the house.

"Poor Mr. Greenthumb," groaned the mayor. "Oh, if only one of us had a green thumb, we could save his little flower."

The sun set. The little flower's head drooped lower.

Suddenly Joseph, the doctor's son, shouted, "I can do it. I can save the little flower!"

"You can *what?*" said the mayor.

"*I think I can save the little flower!*" repeated Joseph. "I have been watching Mr. Greenthumb take care of that flower every day since he came here. I know exactly what to do:

"PFFF! PFFF! PFFF!

"WIPE! WIPE! WIPE!

"SPRINKLE! SPRINKLE! SPRINKLE!"

"It won't work," said a father. "He doesn't have a green thumb."

"WELL AT LEAST HE HAS AN IDEA!" the mayor roared. "Go on, Joseph, give it a try. Green thumb or *no* green thumb."

Joseph took a deep breath and moved toward the sick little flower. With three whispering puffs he blew at the dust on its petals. Not all the dust came off.

Joseph blew harder. A petal blew off the flower.

"Oh!" gasped the mayor.

"Shhh!" scolded the children.

"It's too dark," said Joseph. "I need light."

Six fathers lit the mining lamps on their caps and gathered around the flower. Joseph stuck his hand out.

"HANDKERCHIEF!" he called sharply.

The mayor whipped his clean white handkerchief out of his coat pocket and put it into Joseph's hand.

"Handkerchief!" he whispered, craning his neck to see over the six fathers.

Joseph stretched out his hand again. "Watering can!" he ordered.

"Watering can!" echoed the mayor as he ran into the house. In a few moments he returned with the watering can spilling over with fresh cool water.

Joseph took the watering can. It was so quiet everybody could hear the gurgling sound of the thirsty earth drinking the water.

At last, with a deep trembling sigh, Joseph stepped back. The job was finished.

The little flower's pale red petals ·fluttered weakly in the evening breeze. Then the breeze ran away and the little flower stood still. Its head drooped.

"I knew it wouldn't work," grumbled a grown-up.

"What kind of talk is that?" snapped the mayor. "Did you expect the little flower to roar like a tiger lily the minute it had a drink of water? *It takes time!* Now, skedaddle, all of you. Joseph and I will stay and keep a good eye on the little flower."

That night the doctor sat by the side of Mr. Greenthumb's bed and watched Mr. Greenthumb carefully.

And the mayor and Joseph sat by Mr. Greenthumb's window
sill and watched the little red flower carefully.

The next morning, as the sun came up, the whole town gathered in front of Mr. Greenthumb's house. There in the early light were Joseph and the mayor, fast asleep on the window sill.

Slowly and fearfully, everybody looked at the sick little flower. Their eyes popped wide open. It was the most beautiful sight they had ever seen.

The little red flower wasn't sick any more. Its petals were redder than ever and it stood up straight as an arrow.

The next Sunday there was a happy celebration. It was Mr. Greenthumb's first day out of bed. Everybody came to tell him how glad they were.

He sat in a rocking chair and wore a candy-striped bathrobe. Next to him was a long wooden table covered with little flower pots filled with clean black earth. In the middle stood the little red flower.

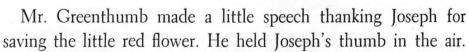
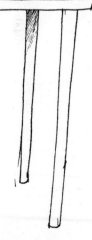

Mr. Greenthumb made a little speech thanking Joseph for saving the little red flower. He held Joseph's thumb in the air.

"And what's more," he added, "he did it without a green thumb!"

"But, Mr. Greenthumb," interrupted Joseph, "what's happened to *your* thumb?"

Mr. Greenthumb lifted his own thumb and stared at it. It wasn't green any more! The green paint had faded completely away!

Mr. Greenthumb chuckled. "Now, what do you suppose THAT proves?" he asked his friends.

"Why," said the mayor, "it just proves you don't need a green thumb to grow *anything*."

"And that," he added importantly, "is a *scientific fact!*"

Still chuckling, Mr. Greenthumb walked over to the long wooden table and picked up a flower pot.

"In each one of these pots," he announced, "is a little red flower seed. Now, who would like to grow a little red flower all his own?"

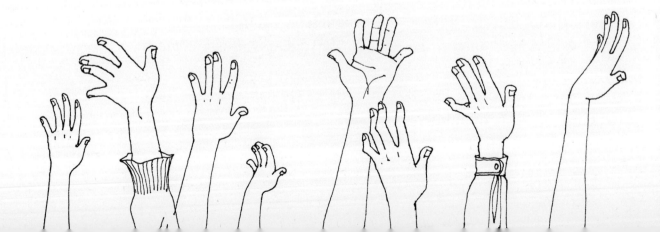

The children gathered in front of the long wooden table and
Mr. Greenthumb gave each boy and girl a little flower pot.

One by one they said, "Thank you," and took their little
flower pots home.
   Then each child put his little flower pot on his window sill,
poured water into it and waited for a little red flower to grow.

Today there is a little red flower on every window sill in the town.

It is still a very dusty town.

It is also a very happy town.

ABOUT THE AUTHOR

This is the second book by one of America's outstanding children's entertainers. Paul Tripp's gift for delighting the young first found expression in *Tubby the Tuba*, the immensely popular album that he wrote and recorded.

From records Mr. Tripp moved to the stage and then to television, with his award-winning program *Mr. I. Magination*—a weekly musical fantasy for children that is considered one of the classics of the television medium. That was followed by *On the Carousel* and most recently by *Birthday House*, a daily TV program that enchanted children for five years.

Meanwhile Mr. Tripp wrote his first book and ventured into films for children with *The Christmas That Almost Wasn't*, which he not only wrote but also starred in.

Mr. Tripp is married to actress Ruth Enders, who has appeared with him in all of his television and film work. They have two children, and live in New York City.

ABOUT THE ILLUSTRATOR

Trina Schart Hyman was born in Philadelphia and grew up in a rural community north of that city. She attended art school in Philadelphia and at the Boston Museum School. And during a year that she lived in Stockholm, she attended the Swedish state art school and illustrated her first children's book for a Swedish publisher.

Since returning to this country Mrs. Hyman has illustrated some twelve books for American publishers. She now lives in New Hampshire in a 200-year-old house that faces the Connecticut River, where she bicycles, hikes, and gardens— when she isn't busy illustrating books and looking after a very young daughter.